This book is dedicated to my siblings, for making me fear less, if not fearless; and to my children, for making me brave.

Charlie the Fearless And Tancho the Brave

Written by
Suhmayah Banda

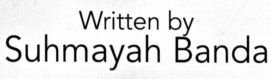

Illustrated by
Sarah-Leigh Wills

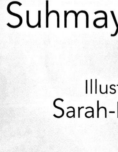

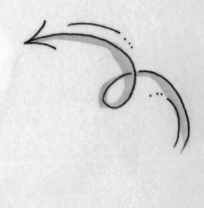

Tancho and Charlie were brothers and best friends.
They liked doing everything together.

They played on the jungle gym together.

They played ball together.

They rode their bikes together.

They did everything together.

The difference was that Charlie was fearless
and sometimes Tancho was scared.

When they were climbing, Charlie climbed
right up to the top but Tancho stopped halfway.

"Don't you want to climb up here?" asked Charlie.

"Not if I don't have to. I'm scared of falling!" said Tancho.

"You're always scared. I'm Charlie the Fearless,
I'm not scared of anything!" Charlie always replied.

Sometimes, while playing ball outside, the neighbor's dog climbed over the fence and into their garden to join them. Tancho didn't like dogs, so he ran inside while Charlie took the dog back next door.

"Don't you want to say hi to Ragnar?" asked Charlie.

"Not really. I'm scared of being bitten," said Tancho.

"You're always scared. I'm Charlie the Fearless,
I'm not scared of anything!" Charlie always replied.

When they rode their bikes uphill,
Charlie sped down the other side as quickly
as he could. Tancho was a little scared of going
too fast, so he followed behind more slowly.

"Don't you want to speed down, like me?"
asked Charlie.

"Not if I don't have to. I'm scared I'll lose my balance,"
said Tancho.

"You're always scared. I'm Charlie the Fearless,
I'm not scared of anything!" Charlie always replied.

One day they were on the jungle gym. Charlie was
at the top as usual and Tancho was halfway up. On the way
down, Charlie's shirt got caught on the climbing frame.
He couldn't move up or down. He was stranded and became
very worried.

As soon as Tancho saw that Charlie was upset, he zoomed
up to the top of the jungle gym to help.

As they made their way back down,
Charlie realized Tancho had climbed right to the top.

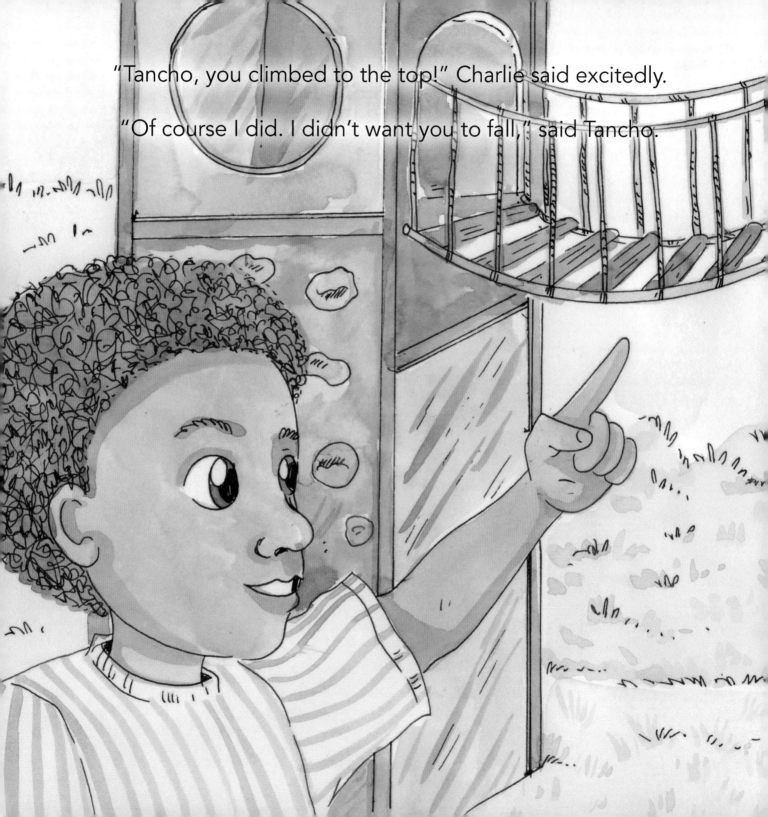

"Tancho, you climbed to the top!" Charlie said excitedly.

"Of course I did. I didn't want you to fall," said Tancho.

Charlie smiled. It made him happy
to know his brother was so brave.

The next day, Tancho and Charlie were playing catch in the park. Tancho threw the ball to Charlie. A dog behind Charlie saw the ball soaring through the air and wanted to play, too. It began running toward Charlie, barking loudly.

Tancho saw the dog and became very worried. He started running as fast as he could and stopped suddenly behind Charlie to shield him from the dog. The dog leaped onto Tancho and started licking his face playfully.

"Tancho, you didn't run away from the dog!" said Charlie in amazement.

"Of course not. I didn't want it to bite you," said Tancho.

Charlie smiled. It made him happy to know his brother was so brave.

A few days later on a bike ride, they came to the top of a steep hill. Charlie started zooming down while Tancho followed behind a little more slowly.

Near the bottom of the hill, Charlie fell off his bike. Tancho, seeing what had happened and hearing Charlie's cry, released the brakes and pedaled downhill as fast as he could to make sure his brother was okay.

Charlie watched in amazement as his brother rocketed down the hill and skidded to a stop beside him. Tancho helped him over to a bench as they waited for Mom and Dad to catch up.

"I've never seen you ride so quickly!" said Charlie.

"I had to, I was worried you had hurt yourself," said Tancho.

Charlie smiled. It made him happy to know his brother was so brave.

One day they went to a theme park. Charlie wanted to go on the new Zero G Slide.

It was very big and very steep.

"It looks very high and very fast.
Are you sure you won't be scared?" asked Mom.

"I'm Charlie the Fearless, I'm not scared of anything!
I also know Tancho the Brave will be there if I need help!"

Tancho smiled. He liked his new name and it made him happy to know that his fearless brother thought he was brave.

Charlie the Fearless
And Tancho the Brave

ISBN: 978-1-9993478-0-2

The moral right of the author has been asserted.

Illustration and design by Sarah-Leigh Wills.
www.happydesigner.co.uk

Printed in Poland
by Amazon Fulfillment
Poland Sp. z o.o., Wrocław